Where Are The Praying Mothers?

By Mikel Brown

CJC Publishing Company

Where Are The Praying Mothers?

Mikel Brown
CJC Publishing Company
1208 Sumac Drive
El Paso, TX. 79925

Copyright © 2002 by Mikel Brown
Printed in the United States of America
Library of Congress Control Number: 2002109486
ISBN: 1-930388-05-5

Editorial assistance for CJC Publishing Co. by CJC editorial Dept.

Cover design by Scott Whittle.

All scripture references are quoted from the King James Version of the Holy Bible unless otherwise noted.

CONTENTS

Dedication

This book is dedicated to all the praying women who have prayed for me and aided in helping me to fulfill my purpose. To the precious women of God who have passed on to be with Jesus and who adopted me as their son. To the aging and young women who are still around today; Please Do not Stop praying! We as men need your prayers and your perseverance. And to the prayer warriors who intercede for their pastors who desperately need to be blanketed with prayer. Thank you for fighting for your sons and daughters.

Preface

As I consider the broad picture of life and all of its complexities, I would be remiss if I did not share on the purpose of assigned prayer for this exact purpose. Life is full of twists and turns, ups and downs, and ins and outs. One moment your marriage can be going well and then, seemingly in a moment's time, it appears to be standing on shifting sand. Situations such as this one can keep you puzzled and confused. There are times when your prayers can break through the clouds, then through the universe, and then ultimately into the third heaven where God resides, and you feel this overwhelming sense of assurance. Other times you can pray and it appears as if your prayers hit the ceiling and bounce back and you do not feel as if you have broken through. In general, life is unpredictable but yet controllable. Paul said that Christians do not know how to pray as they should, but that the Holy Spirit makes intercession for us with groanings which can not be uttered. Since the Holy Spirit knows the mind of God, He knows how God wants us to pray. As you pray in the Holy Spirit, you will discover that your prayers are more accurate and deliberate. The Holy Spirit will assign prayers to certain saints because He is fully aware of the plan of God and the areas that God desires to be targeted in prayer. Therefore, do not become bent out of shape because your prayer agenda seems to be hit and miss. As you learn to pray in the Holy Spirit, His radar system will never miss its target. In spite of life's complexities, continue to pray and you will find that your prayers will hit their target whether you feel like they did or not. Women have the greatest influence on the earth and in the heavens.

1 Peter 3:7 Likewise, ye husbands, dwell with them according to knowledge, giving honour unto the wife, as unto the weaker vessel, and as being heirs together of the grace of life; that your prayers be not hindered.

Although the man is the head of the woman, the head must receive its information through some media source. The woman is the helper to aid the man in defeating his ultimate challenge to crush Satan's head and subdue all things.

Chapter 1

Where Are The Praying Mothers?

Chapter 1

Where Are the Praying Mothers?

"Mama, Mama," cried the troubled child. Mother ran to her child's bedroom to see what was the matter. She placed her hand on the child's head and noticed that he had a fever. She immediately cuddled him in her comforting arms and cried out to God. "O' Lord bless my child and take away this fever. Mommy's right here," she said.

Mothers, and women in general, have always played such a significant and influential role in providing material to the writers of history. God has strategically placed women in the forefront along side the men in every major, and even in the least important events. From Eve in the book of Genesis to the Woman in the book of Revelation, you can literally view the impact of one of God's greatest creations the Mother, the Woman.

A woman has unequivocally influenced every human who has ever lived on this planet in one way or another. There is something unique about women who have experienced motherhood that causes their intrinsic motherly care to surface. Their touch, loving voice, and smile that says, "I love you" without ever opening their mouths can never be achieved or duplicated by a man. A pastor friend of mine once said that he usually asks for a female waitress when visiting any restaurant because a man is unable to cater to his needs like most women can.

I believe that God calls women from all walks of life who are obedient to Him to pray for people who they may not know. I can recall a childhood friend of mine who I felt had the meanest mother in the world. My thoughts concerning her were not prompted by bad treatment, but by the fact that she felt that I was a bad influence on her son. In retrospect, he was a bad influence on me, but most mothers would like to think the best concerning their children. She would say to her sons, "Whatever you do, get that boy in church." This lady knew that my mother was not a regular church attendee, so she focused in on her sons asking my mother to allow me to attend church with them in Momence, Illinois. It was during this time that I experienced a real encounter with the power of prayer. My friend's grandmother, "Big Mama", was the church mother and she embraced me as if I was a part of the family. Prayer was Big Mama's specialty and she was full of compassion, love, and power. It was at this time that I gained a respect for my friend's mother because she prayed for me and was responsible for my initial meeting with God.

One day I was praying and the Lord brought to my attention all the women who were raised up by God to pray. And the question came to my mind, "Where are all the praying Mothers?" I believe God was asking me this question for a reason, because there is a void or gap in the universe that the prayers of women once filled. When I repeated the question, "Where are all the praying Mothers?" I heard a voice so clearly and distinctively. "They are working. They are making a living!" God replied.

12

The enemy (Satan) has succeeded in pushing the women out of the sanctuaries of their homes and into the work force. These women are now off their knees and on their feet for eight to twelve hours a day, leaving the home front defenseless. After working a full time job, most women are too tired to pray. One woman said, "I have just enough strength to cook my children a meal, make sure they bathe, and then crawl into the bed." It is sad that the sacrificial level of most women today is not present. If you do not have time to target your prayer life, you will find that it is easy for Satan to target your life and hit it every time.

Allow me to relate back to the sixties, a time when everything in society was being questioned. The Jim Crowe law of "separate but equal" was under tremendous scrutiny by the NAACP and SCLC. White Americans who did not openly support segregation said very little for fear of their own lives. Crimes were gradually increasing in every community. You may remember the story of Richard Speck who was on the run in Chicago for the brutal murder of eight nursing students. The Mafia was using terrorist tactics to hold businesses hostage in many major American cities. John F. Kennedy was shot and killed in Dallas, Texas, as we watched American citizens mourn the death of its nation's leader. Martin Luther King was assassinated in Memphis, Tennessee while on his way to rally for under paid and unfair treatment of sanitation workers. The United States became more divided at this time than during the Civil War.

With the Equal Rights Amendment and the unfair treatment of women in the work force, this final string would literally loosen the fabric of the American culture. Madalyn Murray O'Hair was the main advocate who was responsible for nudging prayer out of the public schools. It was around this time when women began to flood the work place. As the Lord was speaking to my heart about the absence of praying women, my mind went back to the television shows of the fifties and early sixties. Television shows like the long running series Father Knows Best, The Donna Reed Show, My Three Sons, and Leave it to Beaver were just a few. When these shows left prime time television, it marked the beginning of a major paradigm shift in American history. Replacement shows were reflecting the direction of the American public with their subtle messages that lacked in morality and pointed towards the moral decay in our nation.

While America was at war during World War II, the women were filling the labor force to provide

14

much needed supplies for the American Troops. After the war, as the men returned home, this nation experienced a baby boom and most of the women returned to their homes as the men went out to find work. The absence of prayer became so prevalent that most people were oblivious to what had truly happened that caused this nation to change forever. America's sons began packing our prison systems at record numbers. Our sons and daughters walked out of their closets of homosexuality. The victims of pornography went from women to men to children, and now includes animals. Child pornography increased and crimes against children were embarrassingly high for a nation whose anthem is "God Bless America."

From Rap to Rock, today's music is an open defiance against women and the establishment of the home. The killing of thirteen teens at the Columbine High School in Littleton, Colorado is the end of a trail of cause and effect that leads back to the absence of prayer in the home. The boys who committed these senseless and horrendous murders did not have praying mothers. African American and Latino gang members usually live in communities where there is a church on practically every corner, and yet the influence of the church is absent from their homes. Babies are having babies; siblings are molesting and raping their own flesh and blood. The list of ridiculous crimes and stupid choices made by both youths and adults are ruining the future of many would-be doctors, lawyers, scientists, ministers, inventors, etc. Where are the praying women?

Since the 1950's, when women began flooding the work place, there has been a disturbing increase of crimes against women. The number of women leaving their children after experiencing a divorce has considerably increased. Homosexuality in America has now become a standard preference. Recent reports revealed that a shocking fifty-percent of young high school students who are sexually active have confessed to experimenting in bi-sexual relationships. By the time the United States Supreme Court voted prayer out of our public schools, prayer had already started seeping out of American homes. The framework of this nation was established on the knees of praying women while fathers and sons went off to war. What the woman's prayer means to the man is the same as what Moses' hands lifted on the mountain meant to the Israelites fighting in the valley.

There is something extraordinary about a woman's prayers. Today's women are too tired to pray and too busy to do what God has assigned for them. Satan has succeeded in misdirecting the woman's purpose by getting her off of her knees and on to her feet. The woman has taken unto herself the curse that God has placed on the man, which is to work by the sweat of his brow. I am not at all saying that women should not work; however, if the man is fulfilling his assignment to work and the woman is also out working, then who's left to re-enforce the home and cover the family with prayer? The situation leaves "latchkey" children to prepare their own meals and secure their own homes. The television has become the active parent for many children who rarely see their real parents. How can we maneuver the next generation in the direction of prayer without the woman's help? I submit to you that this cannot and will not be performed until the woman wakes up to the urgency of the moment. The Esther spirit must return and the women must come to realize that God has raised them up for such a time as this. "If I perish, let me perish, I am going to see the king," said Esther. My question is simple. Who will go to the King on our behalf?

I can hear the old Praying Mothers as they "send up timber" for their children and their children's children. Sending up timber is a maxim used to indicate prayer. When women pray, God listens. Down through history, God has placed women in the

17

birth (prayer) position to petition for many things that God wanted to happen on earth. Anna, the prophetess, was just one of the many important women of the scriptures who was used to pray God's will on the earth. This woman was used to pray in the temple day and night until Jesus showed up in the temple for circumcision.

> *Luke 2:36 (KJS)* And there was one Anna, a prophetess, the daughter of Phanuel, of the tribe of Aser: she was of a great age, and had lived with an husband seven years from her virginity;
> 37 And she [was] a widow of about fourscore and four years, which departed not from the temple, but served [God] with fastings and prayers night and day.

This eighty-four year old woman understood her assignment and was willing to forego her youth and opportunity for remarriage after the death of her husband. I am certain that Anna, the prophetess, perhaps entertained the thought of another husband, of having children, and of living in her own home. Yet she chose to remain in a spiritual place of prominence until the Messiah was born. The qualification of Anna to declare words over the life of

Jesus was not that she was a prophetess, but that she was a praying woman. Titles mean nothing without a titleholder to fulfill that which constitutes the designation. The eligibility and endowment for her high calling came because she prayed in the only house where the Son of God was to be circumcised, and declared the purpose of God's house.

Chapter 2

The Seed's Power Source

Chapter 2

The Seed's Power Source

The Mother is the enforcer of the home and if she does not enforce her home with prayer, it leaves the seed (children) vulnerable and without a power source. Women are so vital to what God is doing in the last days that Satan's main thrust is to get the women off of their knees so that the men will stay on theirs. What I mean by this is that as long as the man continues to submit to and be enslaved by pornography, drugs, anger, and uncontrollable cravings, this will be, in part, because the woman has not submitted to her role as intercessor and prayer warrior. When the woman gets back on her knees, the man will have the power to get up and shake off the chain of oppression that has spiritually and mentally enslaved him. I believe that when this happens, we will see men rise up out of their stupor as a result of mothers who fervently pray for their sons and daughters.

Most men realize and recognize how powerful the woman is when she prays. God made the woman strong because only a strong woman can submit to a man and not depreciate her own value. The woman was created to submit to the man. This simply means that she is designed to get under him and aid him in fulfilling his purpose. God said that it was not good that man was alone. Man needed a suitable helper because what God assigned for the man could not be accomplished in the physical state of being all one.

The story I am about to tell you is true and no part of it is fabricated to validate my point. There was a man convicted of murder who had escaped from prison and broken into the home of an eighty-year-old woman. He was about to hold this seemingly defenseless old woman hostage except that she looked at him and said, "I am a godly woman and you are not going to come into my house and hold me

22

hostage. If you want something to eat, I will prepare something for you to eat." The escaped murderer looked into the eyes of this woman and saw that she had no fear of him. She told him that she would pray for him. She prepared a meal for him and as he started to eat she said vehemently, "Son, pray over your food!" "I don't know how to pray," said the escaped convict. The precious woman said, "I will teach you how to pray." She told him what to say and the man repeated the prayer and ate his food. It was during the course of that same day that this convicted murderer, who had escaped from prison, gave his life to the Lord and later turned himself in to the authorities. I believe that it was God's divine intention to aid in this man's escape from prison, only for him to run into the presence of a praying woman.

There is not a man alive who has affected my life more than the praying women who embraced me as their son in the gospel and poured into me the spirit of prayer. I am not suggesting that men have done little or nothing for me throughout my years of ministry because they have done much. That subject is another book in the making. I did not learn how to pray from a textbook of prayers; I did not learn how to pray in the presence of men; I learned how to pray in the presence of praying women. I received Jesus Christ as my Lord and Savior during a Sunday morning service while attending Prayer Tower COGIC. Old and gray haired women took me into the basement of the church and spilled God's word into my heart. They fed me and kept me in the basement of this church until the evening service began. I did not have the guts to say to these women that I wanted to go home. The following day, a week long revival was to commence. I had no plans to attend this event, but these mothers had other plans. They forced me to commit to coming to the revival and made sure that I had a ride every night. I was under the assumption that the time I would arrive at the church would be the beginning of the actual revival service, but much to my surprise, the only people present at the time I arrived were about 7 to 10 old women praying. I found myself in the midst of an hour long prayer as they were praying for the revival meeting. One woman called me to the altar and made me stay by her while she prayed, and it was at this time that a "Praying Spirit" was imparted in me. What started out for me as laborious and tedious prayers, ended in joyful delight. For five days we prayed for the revival, and during these powerful prayer meetings I became pregnant with a prayer purpose.

The book of Genesis is noted as the book of beginnings. It is within the pages of this first book that we see the origin of life, the first marriage, the first sin, the first murder, the first rainbow, and many other first occurrences as well. After Adam and Eve had sinned and God handed out retribution, we see man's sin consciousness come into effect. When men and women refuse to accept responsibility for their actions and hide instead of confronting it, this is the sin consciousness in action. As this situation unfolded, Satan was handed keys to the earth system and he commenced to dominate the world.

> *Gen 3:11 (KJS)* And he said, Who told thee that thou [wast] naked? Hast thou eaten of the tree, whereof I commanded thee that thou shouldest not eat?
> 12 And the man said, The woman whom thou gavest [to be] with me, she gave me of the tree, and I did eat.
> 13 And the LORD God said unto the woman, What [is] this [that] thou hast done? And the woman said, The serpent beguiled me, and I did eat.

Notice in verses eleven and twelve that God addresses the man about eating from the forbidden tree. The reason God addressed the Man first was because he was created first and was given all the instructions from God. Adam was the leader, teacher, and head. Adam lost his position when he refused to accept responsibility for his actions and he accredited his error to his wife. Then God addressed the woman and she blamed her sin on Satan. Consequently, the authority that was originally given to Adam had been passed to the woman and then to Satan. Eve proclaimed, "The Devil made me do it!" Flip Wilson, the late comedian, played a character by the name of "Geraldine" who made this line famous. The original person responsible for the line "The devil made me do it!" was not Geraldine; it was Eve. Adam and Eve were the initiators of what is commonly known today as "Shifting the Blame."

14 And the LORD God said unto the serpent, Because thou hast done this, thou [art] cursed above all cattle, and above every beast of the field; upon thy belly shalt thou go, and dust shalt thou eat all the days of thy life:
15 And I will put enmity between thee and the woman, and between thy seed and her seed; it shall bruise thy head, and thou shalt bruise his heel.
16 Unto the woman he said, I will greatly multiply thy sorrow and thy conception; in sorrow thou shalt bring forth children; and thy desire [shall be] to thy husband, and he shall rule over thee.
17 And unto Adam he said, Because thou hast hearkened unto the voice of

thy wife, and hast eaten of the tree, of which I commanded thee, saying, Thou shalt not eat of it: cursed the ground for thy sake; in sorrow shalt thou eat it all the days of thy life;

18 Thorns also and thistles shall it bring forth to thee; and thou shalt eat the herb of the field;

19 In the sweat of thy face shalt thou eat bread, till thou return unto the ground; for out of it wast thou taken: for dust thou [art], and unto dust shalt thou return.

As you read verses fourteen through nineteen you will see that God began passing out restitution in the order of authority. Satan, the woman, and then the man, was the sequence of improperly delegated authority. Satan would never have any authority over the earth and the lives of people if Adam would have faced his error and turned to God. Instead, Adam used the woman as an excuse and made God accountable for his actions by saying to God "the woman you gave to me." Therefore, God placed the woman in the position of the initiator with Satan.

The word *enmity* in verse fifteen does not simply mean hatred. There is much more to the meaning of this word. The English language does not transliterate it properly. The word that is more appropriate to use in verse fifteen, is "feud." Consequently, God is saying I will put a feud between thee and the woman, and between thy seed and her seed. The end result will be that her feud will fuel her seed to bruise Satan's head. The best that Satan's seed will do to the seed of the woman is bruise the heel of his foot, but his foot will crush Satan's head. God did not simply place within the woman hatred or animosity against Satan, but rather a warring spirit between her and the Serpent.

The first war declared on planet earth was not against Satan and the Man. The first acknowledged war was between the Woman and the Serpent. Are you reading the same King James Bible that I am? This event is clearly stated. God is the one declaring the war and He has established a natural feud between this powerful woman (whom the Bible calls the weaker vessel) and Satan (who likes to think of himself as a dominate force).

If the woman does not adhere to her instinctive feud, then her seeds (children) will pick up the very things that caused her to fall. The serpent exposed the woman's hidden desire by informing her of what the fruit could provide. How could someone convince another person to want something that they already had, unless the person did not recognize that they originally had it? To be like God was a strange

28

temptation for the woman because she was already like God. Her desire to be someone other than who she already was became the temptation that caused her to reach for and desire a fruit that was off limits. The fruit that caused her disruptive appetite became the very fruit that her first son offered to God as a sacrifice, which God rejected. The seed of the parent's rebellion and/or obedience is wrapped within the fabric of the seeds.

Notice that the scriptures give attention to one war, but different battles. The woman's feud against the serpent is the first battle and the second battle is between her seed and Satan's seed. In other words, the destiny of the woman and the serpent is also the destiny of their seed. Therefore, whatever occurs between the woman and the serpent will occur with their seed. The woman is the carrier of the seed. God has assigned her to give everything required to the unborn child in order to prepare him or her to develop enough strength to pass through the birth canal without being crushed. Satan's main interest is not in the seed, but in the source from which the seed will receive the power to crush his head. If the woman does not intercede for the man (seed), the man will not have enough power to kick a flea.

The word "bruise" mentioned in verse 15

literally means to come down with a force, to crush. If the woman does not fulfill her role to engage in a feud with Satan and to intercede for the man, he will not possess enough force in his legs to crush Satan's head. The prayer of the woman will fuel the man in his battle against the seed of Satan. The man and the woman must team up together in order to overcome Satan and his schemes. When the home is an environment of prayer, the environment will eventually influence the man to fight the devil with determination.

Chapter 3

Praying Women Refuse To Settle

Chapter 3

Praying Women Refuse to Settle

Jesus taught the disciples about perseverance by telling a story about a woman and a judge. On many occasions in the Bible, Jesus' lesson plans included women who were able to break through the most difficult of circumstances and receive answers to their prayers. Why are there so many stories about praying women in the Bible if God never intended for the woman to be the dominate intercessor?

I greatly admire the woman's ability to endure

pain and agony. Any woman who can carry another human being inside her body for nine months and go through excruciating pain before and during delivery, has my greatest respect. Aretha Franklin once said, "All she wanted was a little respect." I greatly respect and honor the woman and her potential to endure most anything. Most men would never be willing to experience a second pregnancy after the delivery of the first child because men have a low threshold for pain. Men also have little tolerance for rejection. I am the first to admit that if I am not feeling well, I want my wife to baby me. I need the affirmation from my wife that I am not going to die from a headache. (Smile) My experience as a child was that my Mother was the only sympathizer when I was ill. My stepfather had neither the concern nor the patience to labor with me until I became well. My Mother would bring up hot soup and a sandwich when I was not feeling well. My stepfather would say that there was nothing wrong with me and that she should not be attending to me like I was a baby.

The Bible gives to us a treasure hidden in the scriptures, about a praying mother and an intelligent wife. This woman was referred to as the Shunammite woman. She was both sensitive and attentive to the need of Elisha, the man of God. She influenced her husband to build a penthouse for Elisha so that he would have a place to stay whenever he passed through their country. By doing this, she secured the blessings of God on their household and their business. She must have been a good wife. She was also intelligent in the way she communicated to her husband. Other than the fact that Elisha was a man of God, her husband had to have confidence in her judgment to build a penthouse for a man he knew nothing about This shows the power and influence of a virtuous woman. One day, Elisha prophesied that the Shunammite woman would have a child and it happened exactly as the man of God spoke it. She no longer struggled with having children, as she had done for so long, because her act of love towards the man of God untangled her fight and opened her womb. As the child grew older the Bible says that the child, who was with his father at the time, complained of a headache.

> *2Kin 4:18 (KJS)* And when the child was grown, it fell on a day, that he went out to his father to the reapers.
> 19 And he said unto his father, My head, my head. And he said to a lad, Carry him to his mother.

There are two important aspects concerning the

father's reaction that I would like to point out. First, when the child complained that his head was hurting, the father was not concerned enough to investigate the seriousness of his son's complaint. Second, instead of caring for the boy himself, he sent his son to his Mother. Perhaps he was thinking that the boy was trying to get out of work, which is typical of how most men think. This Shunammite woman understood and respected the price she had to pay to birth her son and she was not going to allow her son to be taken from her without a fight. Men can learn a lot from their wives when it comes to praying for their children. As men become older and tainted by the world's system, their sensitivity level begins to dwindle. Women become stronger in spiritual matters if they continue to be diligent in seeking the face of God while men grow more insensitive.

> *2Kin 4:20 (KJS)* And when he had taken him, and brought him to his mother, he sat on her knees till noon, and died.

The mother took her son and placed him in her lap and started praying. I can recall as a child, during one of my episodes of illness, my young mother had me on her knees as she cried and prayed for me. She was not a confessing Christian at the time, but she was a loving mother. As soon as she spoke that I would be all right, I felt a sense of security and relief. My wellness came because of her comforting words. The Shunammite woman believed in the anointing God placed in Elisha, and when her son died, the prophet was the first thought on her mind. She did not bother with making funeral arrangements or even informing her husband. She knew that he would only discourage her from doing what she knew had to be done.

> *2Kin 4:21 (KJS)* **And she went up, and laid him on the bed of the man of God, and shut [the door] upon him, and went out.**
> **22 And she called unto her husband, and said, Send me, I pray thee, one of the young men, and one of the asses, that I may run to the man of God, and come again.**
> **23 And he said, Wherefore wilt thou go to him to day? [it is] neither new moon, nor sabbath. And she said, [It shall be] well.**
> **24 Then she saddled an ass, and said to her servant, Drive, and go forward; slack not [thy] riding for me, except I bid thee.**
> **25 So she went and came unto the man of God to mount Carmel. And it came**

36

to pass, when the man of God saw her afar off, that he said to Gehazi his servant, Behold, [yonder is] that Shunammite:

This woman's act of faith is demonstrative of the feud that God placed in all women. Her husband could not figure out why she was so interested in seeing the man of God when it was not a Sabbath or a New Moon. When asked by her husband why she wanted a donkey to go to the man of God, she simply replied, "It shall be well." She did not allow the death of her son to settle with her. Determined and armed with a fury, she was spurred on to drive forward in order to ensure that her seed would live again. She never spoke a negative word concerning her situation. She did not undermine her husband because she realized that it was her responsibility to fuel the seed with her feud against wickedness. Sickness is stolen health; poverty is stolen wealth; and death is stolen life. What a powerful woman who chose not to belabor her husband with matters she proclaimed would be well. This kind of fight and belief in the power of God is missing in most Christian women today. You must be able to see that it was a necessity that she avoid telling her husband about a problem that she had determined to take care of. If a woman is preparing a meal for her husband and the meat is overcooked, she should not have to call him at work and inform him of something that she can easily take care of herself. The woman who faithfully cares for her home would simply trash the meat gone bad and quickly prepare another main dish without the man's knowledge of what went wrong. The man would come home, eat what was prepared and set before him, and never realize that he was eating a second choice meal. He would not be interested in the particulars; he would just want to eat when he came home. When a man is gone off to war, he can take comfort in knowing that his wife loves him, is praying for him, and is caring for their children. But if the soldier has to worry about home, it is because he knows that the woman he married is not a faithful trustee over his affairs.

> *2Kin 4:27 (KJS)* And when she came to the man of God to the hill, she caught him by the feet: but Gehazi came near to thrust her away. And the man of God said, Let her alone; for her soul [is] vexed within her: and the LORD hath hid [it] from me, and hath not told me.
> 28 Then she said, Did I desire a son of my lord? did I not say, Do not deceive me?
> 29 Then he said to Gehazi, Gird up thy loins, and take my staff in thine hand, and go thy way: if thou meet any man,

salute him not; and if any salute thee,
answer him not again: and lay my staff
upon the face of the child.
30 And the mother of the child said,
[As] the LORD liveth, and [as] thy soul
liveth, I will not leave thee. And he
arose, and followed her.

What the Shunammite woman was willing to do
was what her husband would have felt humiliated to
do. She realized that her son's life was on the line,
not her pride. She needed a miracle, and she realized
that being prideful would hinder the process of
receiving the miracle that she needed. This woman
pleaded her case by saying, "I did not ask for a child.
And I asked you not to deceive me and give me
something that would only crush me."
(Paraphrased) She could not accept the fact that
God would give her something that would later be
taken away by death. The Shunammite woman
displayed an intuitive thought that the spiritual was
greater than the physical. This woman fought death
by going to the one who spoke her child into her
womb. She refused to go to the person who was
physically responsible for placing the seed within
her. Her refusal to leave the side of the man of God
until something happened was evidenced by Gehazi
(the prophet's assistant) having to pass them up to do

what the prophet had sent him to perform.

31 And Gehazi passed on before them, and laid the staff upon the face of the child; but [there was] neither voice, nor hearing. Wherefore he went again to meet him, and told him, saying, The child is not awaked.

32 And when Elisha was come into the house, behold, the child was dead, [and] laid upon his bed.

33 He went in therefore, and shut the door upon them twain, and prayed unto the LORD.

34 And he went up, and lay upon the child, and put his mouth upon his mouth, and his eyes upon his eyes, and his hands upon his hands: and he stretched himself upon the child; and the flesh of the child waxed warm.

35 Then he returned, and walked in the house to and fro; and went up, and stretched himself upon him: and the child sneezed seven times, and the child opened his eyes.

36 And he called Gehazi, and said, Call this Shunammite. So he called her. And when she was come in unto him, he said, Take up thy son.

37 Then she went in, and fell at his feet, and bowed herself to the ground, and took up her son, and went out.

When death arrives, it is when the doctor has met his match. With Jesus, however, death can come but it must go when we place matters into the hands of the Master. Can you imagine the father returning home and asking his wife, "Why did you go to the man of God?" She would reply, "Our son died, and I wanted the man of God to come and heal him because he was responsible for the miracle. I figured that if it took a miracle to birth a son, it would take a miracle to keep him." Most likely, the father would wrestle with whether or not to believe her story, seeing his son sitting at the dining table with them. The Shunammite woman understood that it was not important that he believed her, what was important was that all was well when he returned home.

We need women praying for the sons and daughters of the church. Women are needed to cover the men in prayer while they are at war against the devil. I don't care if all women filled my prayer meetings. Just give me some women with a fight in them and together we can turn our city around for Jesus. While the women watched Jesus during his crucifixion and were the first at the tomb after He rose from the dead, the men were out running and hiding. Mary showed up at the tomb early in the morning and Jesus rewarded her by showing Himself to her. Before any of the disciples saw Jesus,

He was seen by a woman who went seeking her Master. Thank God for women who rise early in the mornings to call on God on behalf of their family, pastor, church, and community. It is this kind of sacrifice that God honors and rewards.

Chapter 4

The Persistence of a Praying Woman

Chapter 4

The Persistence of a Praying Woman

I do not believe that anyone would disagree with the fact that a woman can be very persistent when it comes to getting what she wants. Where men are unwilling to explore is where most women will excel. As I mentioned in the previous chapter, the ability in a woman to carry a child nine months and endure the pain of delivery is exemplary. When the woman is ready to deliver the child, this is when her entire psyche changes. The contractions come because an extraction is in the process. The mindset shifts from carrying to delivering. It is important that the woman understands this because her knowledge is key to her purpose. The woman is the quintessential example of the word PUSH (Pray Until Something Happens).

Jesus teaches us about a woman who continued to go before a judge (who had no fear of God) to avenge her of her adversary. The Judge continued to send her away and not hear her case until he became weary of her frequent presence before him with the same case that he continued to dismiss. Her persistence paid off. Eventually, the judge not only heard her case again, but he also did something about it. Jesus uses this as an example of how God will respond because of the constant prayers going before Him, day and night. Praying mothers will not stop until God stops them.

> *Mark 7:25 (KJS)* **For a [certain] woman, whose young daughter had an unclean spirit, heard of him, and came and fell at his feet:**
> **26 The woman was a Greek, a Syrophenician by nation; and she besought him that he would cast forth the devil out of her daughter.**
> **27 But Jesus said unto her, Let the children first be filled: for it is not meet**

45

to take the children's bread, and to cast [it] unto the dogs.

28 And she answered and said unto him, Yes, Lord: yet the dogs under the table eat of the children's crumbs.

29 And he said unto her, For this saying go thy way; the devil is gone out of thy daughter.

30 And when she was come to her house, she found the devil gone out, and her daughter laid upon the bed.

This woman was neither a Jew nor a follower of Christ at the time. She was a woman who happened to be a good mother, concerned about the welfare of her daughter. Some Mothers today have these same problems with their daughters, who may be on drugs, or have run away from home, or may have turned to prostitution. The attitude of this Syrophenician woman was of such precision that it went directly toward the heart of Jesus. God will bite on faith like a fish will bite on bait. Without faith it is impossible to please God, and her faith was impressive. Her daughter was possessed by a demon and she went to Jesus for her daughter to be delivered. She had no intention to leave His presence without His assurance of her daughter's deliverance.

"It is not right for me to give the children's bread to the dog!" said Jesus. How would you personally deal with Jesus making this statement to you? Most men would consider those to be fighting words. Yet this woman responded with such faith and intelligence that Jesus saw that nothing was going to deter her, not even his insults, although Jesus did not intend for it to be an offense. The woman was declaring that the deliverance her daughter needed amounted to nothing more than the crumbs that fell from the abundance of the Master's table. In other words, to heal her daughter could not dent Jesus' abundance of riches. Deliverance for her daughter would have never come if the mother did not go to Jesus for answers. Can this kind of faith be found among the women of the church today? The feud must live on in the woman. Therefore, fight for your children, fight for your husbands, fight for your family, and fight for your church!

A passage of scripture in Mark, chapter seven, reveals the influence of the woman. One day Jesus and His disciples were invited to a wedding, which His mother and friends also attended. During the festivities, the wedding host discovered that his guest had depleted his wine supply. Mary, Jesus' mother, asked her son to provide more wine. Jesus' reply was, "My time is not yet!" Mary paid no attention to what Jesus said and even ordered a couple of young men to provide containers of water and said,

"Whatever he tells you to do, do it." Jesus found Himself performing His first recorded miracle after He said that His time had not yet come. Essentially, He told her no, but Mother Mary said yes! Mother Mary's influence moved Jesus, the Son of God, in the direction of her desire.

Chapter 5

The Intrinsic Power of a Woman

Chapter 5

The Intrinsic Power of the Woman

Gen 2:18 And the LORD God said, [It is] not good that the man should be alone; I will make an help meet for him.

God gives the authority to the man to administrate, but he cannot properly direct without the woman. The woman has an innate, deep-seated ability to be the "helper." The words used in the Bible to describe her assignment are *"help meet."* This means one who is suitable or adaptable for the needs of another. God does not give life without first giving purpose for that life. The woman's original design was to be a suitable and adaptable assistant. With the life that God gave to the woman came the authority attached to her design. If you want to destroy the man, you must go after his power source. For this reason, Satan did not initially approach the man to eat from the forbidden tree. Satan indirectly attacked the man by way of the woman. He appealed to the woman's desire to be in control and to be like God. His approach towards the woman was both subtle and calculating. Eve discovered that her desire to be in control caused her to fall out of control. If a woman abuses her privilege of influence by manipulating instead of helping the man, she will find herself dominated by the demonic powers that control her spouse. If Eve had been able to see the depth of her sin before surrendering her husband to the control of Satan, she would have never surrendered her position for no more than a piece of fruit that she never got to enjoy again.

It must be understood that the helper has the greatest influence. When the woman gave the fruit to her husband to eat, she passed her power to influence her husband over to Satan. I am not excusing Adam, who chose to eat of the fruit when he had a choice not to. I am simply demonstrating the abuse of the gift of the woman, which aided in the fall of mankind.

Most Christian and non-Christian men will tell you that though their wives do not have the final say in matters concerning the family, the women do exert the dominate influence. If a man will lie about this, he will lie about other things as well. (Smile) When a man attempts to dominate his spouse, he robs her of her power to help him, and thus continues under the curse that God placed on the couple.

> *Gen 3:16* ...and thy desire [shall be] to thy husband, and he shall rule over thee.

The woman was condemned to a state of sorrow and subjection because she used her anointing (gift) to persuade Adam to eat the forbidden fruit. She was a gift to him, preordained to lift him up, not to bring him down. If Adam and Eve had not sinned, they would have reigned supreme on the earth. Humility and obedience would have been Eve's greatest qualities, and wisdom and love would have served Eve all the days of her life. The sorrow suffered by the woman in childbirth is a constant reminder of how she birthed sin into a previously perfect world. Instead of Adam and Eve giving birth to the purposes of God, the two of them brought forth a sinful humanity of their own kind.

The feud in Genesis 3:15 seems to echo in Abraham's story. Please allow me to expound on this truth. Sarah was the instigator of the Abraham and Hagar saga. She encouraged Abraham to sleep with her servant Hagar and the two of them produced Ishmael who was rejected and dejected by Sarah, even though she arranged for it all to happen. As a result of Sarah's approval of Abraham and Hagar coming together, Hagar began to turn her nose up at Sarah because Sarah did not have a child. Sarah thought that she was helping Abraham produce the child God said they would have, when in fact she aided in producing friction between her seed and the seed of Hagar. I realize that this revelation can be subjective and the imagery can be speculative. Oftentimes, it is difficult to embrace a revelation of truth when what you have been hearing has only been in half-truth. When Paul unveiled revelation about the church, it was not something that everyone embraced. Because of this new church revelation that Paul received from the Lord, doors of equality opened for both Jew and Gentile. Revelation often bridges the gap between one scripture and another.

Abraham typifies God and Adam, who is responsible for the physical existence of Jesus and the spiritual presence of Lucifer. Sarah represented Eve in the Garden of Eden, who produced a seed named Isaac, and Hagar was symbolic of Satan who pushes out of her womb a seed named Ishmael. Genesis 3:15 is being played out again and again throughout the course of history. To this very present day, the Arabs (offspring of Ishmael) and Jews (offspring of Isaac) are in constant conflict. The flesh and the spirit are ever warring for dominance. Isaac is the spiritual offspring of a woman who could have no children and yet at 90 years of age produced a male child. Ishmael is the fleshly offspring of a woman who did not have trouble in producing a male child. Ishmael held bitterness and hatred in his heart against Abraham and his half-brother Isaac. Still, God who gave Ishmael both authority and a kingdom, allowed him to become a mighty nation. This scenario will continue to unfold throughout the years to come until the ultimate Seed meets up in the conflict of the ages with Satan's seed, as it is outlined in the book of Revelation. Do you earnestly believe that Satan can gain power and authority without God delegating it to him? All authority is of God, both spiritual and physical.

I pray that every woman who reads this book is able to see her God given design to exercise power over Satan and to fuel her male counterparts to crush the head of the opposition. I believe that when women begin to fill our churches again to intercede on behalf of the seed, we will see a decline in sin within the church house. The world already has a death sentence on it, but the church that I am concerned about has a life sentence of blessing. Jesus said in His last prayer to the Father that He was not praying for the world, but for those whom He was leaving in the world. The church is the key for the Christian. Jesus said that He was going to build His church and the gates of Hell can not prevail against it. The Church is often symbolically referred to as the bride of Christ. It is within this context that we find that hell cannot overpower it.

Chapter 6

When A Praying Woman Becomes A Mother

Chapter 6

_____

When A Praying Woman Becomes A Mother

There was a man named Elkanah (described in the book of First Samuel) who had two wives. One wife was called Peninnah and the other wife called Hannah. There was nothing in particular that stood out about these two young women, except for a small deficiency in Hannah's ability to have children. Peninnah often provoked Hannah because she was jealous of her. Peninnah was very insecure in her role as a wife of Elkanah, and would oftentimes invalidate Hannah. Peninnah had sons and daughters from Elkanah, but he did not love her like he loved Hannah. The Bible does not emphasize or belabor the point that one woman was more attractive than the other one. The Bible does say that Elkanah loved Hannah and would give to her a double portion of meat while only giving Peninnah and her children a single portion. One thing stands out in contrast about these two women. Hannah often went to the temple to pray, while Peninnah stayed home running her mouth so that she could upset Hannah. Why would a woman who had children be jealous of a woman who could not have children? Jealous people are vicious and are always looking for a reason to invalidate others in order to feel good about themselves. A jealous attitude will always keep others from giving their best to you. A jealous person can have most of what they want, but they find themselves always envious of what someone else has. Elkanah was married to both of them, and yet Peninnah was antagonistic towards Hannah. Although Hannah could have retaliated against Peninnah's wickedness, she chose not to. Character may be down played in our culture today, but it is still an essential quality in the life of a believer. This is especially true if the believer is aware that what is in the parents may eventually be picked up by the children.

> *1Sam 1:6 (KJS)* And her adversary also
> provoked her sore, for to make her fret,
> because the LORD had shut up her
> womb.
> 7 And [as] he did so year by year, when
> she went up to the house of the LORD,
> so she provoked her; therefore she
> wept, and did not eat.

God used a bad situation to drive Hannah into His throne room. She did not know that she would be driven to her knees in order to pray to God for a son. God wanted her to birth a son that He would use for His glory in matters pertaining to His heart. God sometimes chooses to use the ugliness in people who are unwilling to seek Him for help to push out the goodness in others who are willing to offer themselves for His purpose and use. The first chapter of First Samuel emphasizes the faithfulness of Hannah, not the wickedness of Hophni and Phinehas, the two sons of Eli (who were the priest of the Lord). This chapter is about a woman who God wanted to use to birth a prophet, priest and judge who would stand in His position to minister with integrity for God to the people of Israel. God would not consider a woman for this motherly position if she had nothing in her spiritually to pass on to her seed. Hannah had a deep desire to know God and to offer Him what she believed God had given to her.

Timothy was another who had an anointing transferred from his mother and also from his grandmother.

> *2Tim 1:5 (KJS)* When I call to remembrance the unfeigned faith that is in thee, which dwelt first in thy grandmother Lois, and thy mother Eunice; and I am persuaded that in thee also.

In Paul's letter to Timothy (whose mother and grandmother were Jewish believers and whose father was Greek), Paul pointed out that what he had seen operating in the life of Timothy's mother and grandmother, he believed resided in Timothy as well. Notice that Paul gave no attention to the father, other than that he was Greek. (Acts 16:1) These two precious women were referred to as women of faith, not women of gossip and slander. Their faithfulness and loyalty to the gospel of Jesus Christ was tantamount in their service to Paul. Timothy's service toward Paul and the mission laid upon his shoulders echoed the sentiments of his mother and grandmother. Paul was so impressed with the qualities in Timothy that he wanted Timothy to come with him on the mission field. Timothy probably spent a great deal of time in prayer meetings and church services after getting saved. Children usually mimic their parents, or they may be blessed by God giving them the grace to fight off the attributes of their rebellious parents. In any respect, Timothy's spiritual qualities came from his mother and grandmother. Hannah was selected because the attributes that she practiced in her life needed to be present in Samuel's life.

> *1Sam 1:9 (KJS)* So Hannah rose up after they had eaten in Shiloh, and after they had drunk. Now Eli the priest sat upon a seat by a post of the temple of the LORD.
> 10 And she [was] in bitterness of soul, and prayed unto the LORD, and wept sore.
> 11 And she vowed a vow, and said, O LORD of hosts, if thou wilt indeed look on the affliction of thine handmaid, and remember me, and not forget thine handmaid, but wilt give unto thine handmaid a man child, then I will give him unto the LORD all the days of his life, and there shall no razor come upon his head.

Since Hannah was comfortable going to the

temple to pray, she had no second thoughts about the vow she made to God concerning her first born. What she offered to God was what God wanted in exchange for giving her children and a firstborn son. He would open her womb to bring forth a son for His purpose and use. Through her umbilical cord she would transfer to Samuel all of her spiritual qualities and her deep desire to commune with God. Where Hannah would go to pray was where Samuel, her firstborn would end up living.

> *1Sam 1:13 (KJS)* Now Hannah, she spake in her heart; only her lips moved, but her voice was not heard: therefore Eli thought she had been drunken.
> 14 And Eli said unto her, How long wilt thou be drunken? put away thy wine from thee.
> 15 And Hannah answered and said, No, my lord, I [am] a woman of a sorrowful spirit: I have drunk neither wine nor strong drink, but have poured out my soul before the LORD.
> 16 Count not thine handmaid for a daughter of Belial: for out of the abundance of my complaint and grief have I spoken hitherto.
> 17 Then Eli answered and said, Go in peace: and the God of Israel grant [thee] thy petition that thou hast asked of him.

18 And she said, Let thine handmaid find grace in thy sight. So the woman went her way, and did eat, and her countenance was no more [sad].

Her prayer was intense and targeted for results. She may have appeared drunk because, in her praying, she was speaking with a feud in her. Hannah claimed that she was pouring out her soul to the Lord. My question is "What does pouring out your soul to the Lord mean?" I realize that many Christians will pray when they feel a sense of desperation, but God does not normally respond to desperate prayers. God is never under pressure, nor does He respond to deadlines. Why would God care about a person dying when He can bring them back to life? Why would it matter to God if a person lost their sight, when God can give sight to the blind? So what if a person is being pressured by the mortgage company to become current on their mortgage. God can turn your financial situation around in one second. In truth, if He decides not to turn your financial situation around, He can give you favor with the mortgage company. God is not under pressure to respond to us. Hannah was not praying as though she only had a few years left in her to have children. She was only praying what God always wanted for her, which was for her to have children.

"Thy will be done on earth as it is in heaven" was the kind of prayer she was praying. Her desire was God's desire. Pouring out your soul is exposing the God-given desire of your heart. It means to push in prayer and supplication until Heaven responds to your petition. To pour out your soul before the Lord is to lie bare your whole heart and soul. Your entire being expresses itself outwardly, while you are travailing. This kind of prayer is praying until you get through. Elijah himself prayed with this kind of intensity when he was praying for rain.

1Sam 1:20 (KJS) **Wherefore it came to pass, when the time was come about after Hannah had conceived, that she bare a son, and called his name Samuel, [saying], Because I have asked him of the LORD.**
21 And the man Elkanah, and all his house, went up to offer unto the LORD the yearly sacrifice, and his vow.
22 But Hannah went not up; for she said unto her husband, [I will not go up] until the child be weaned, and [then] I will bring him, that he may appear before the LORD, and there abide for ever.
23 And Elkanah her husband said unto her, Do what seemeth thee good; tarry until thou have weaned him; only the LORD establish his word. So the

woman abode, and gave her son suck
until she weaned him.

Hannah called her first born, Samuel, whose
name means "Asked of God." *While Hannah was
asking God for a son, God was asking Hannah for a
servant.* After the child was born, Hannah refused to
return to the temple until she had weaned Samuel.
Elkanah allowed her to do just as she had vowed, and
she kept her vow to God, and God honored her with
more children.

1Sam 1:24 (KJS) **And when she had
weaned him, she took him up with her,
with three bullocks, and one ephah of
flour, and a bottle of wine, and brought
him unto the house of the LORD in
Shiloh: and the child [was] young.
25 And they slew a bullock, and
brought the child to Eli.
26 And she said, Oh my lord, [as] thy
soul liveth, my lord, I [am] the woman
that stood by thee here, praying unto
the LORD.
27 For this child I prayed; and the
LORD hath given me my petition
which I asked of him:
28 Therefore also I have lent him to the
LORD; as long as he liveth he shall be
lent to the LORD. And he worshipped
the LORD there.
2:1 And Hannah prayed, and said, My**

heart rejoiceth in the LORD, mine horn is exalted in the LORD: my mouth is enlarged over mine enemies; because I rejoice in thy salvation.

2 [There is] none holy as the LORD: for [there is] none beside thee: neither [is there] any rock like our God.

3 Talk no more so exceeding proudly; let [not] arrogancy come out of your mouth: for the LORD [is] a God of knowledge, and by him actions are weighed.

4 The bows of the mighty men [are] broken, and they that stumbled are girded with strength.

5 [They that were] full have hired out themselves for bread; and [they that were] hungry ceased: so that the barren hath born seven; and she that hath many children is waxed feeble.

6 The LORD killeth, and maketh alive: he bringeth down to the grave, and bringeth up.

7 The LORD maketh poor, and maketh rich: he bringeth low, and lifteth up.

8 He raiseth up the poor out of the dust, [and] lifteth up the beggar from the dunghill, to set [them] among princes, and to make them inherit the throne of glory: for the pillars of the earth [are] the LORD'S, and he hath set the world upon them.

9 He will keep the feet of his saints, and the wicked shall be silent in darkness; for by strength shall no man prevail.

10 The adversaries of the LORD shall be broken to pieces; out of heaven shall he thunder upon them: the LORD shall judge the ends of the earth; and he shall give strength unto his king, and exalt the horn of his anointed.
11 And Elkanah went to Ramah to his house. And the child did minister unto the LORD before Eli the priest.

In Samuel 1:28 it appears as if she is lending her son to the Lord, however, this is not the case. The words "...as long as he liveth he shall be lent to the Lord" are not meant to leave the impression that Samuel was loaned and not given. In the original Hebrew, the transliteration should read, "He whom I have obtained by petition shall be returned." She was not lending her son to God; she was returning him back to his Creator. Hannah is the epitome of a woman of God who becomes a mother, only to give her child back to God to be used as He pleases. Women today lack this kind of commitment, not only to God, but also to the House of God. Hannah wanted her son to be all that God had brought him into this world to become. She did not sit him down and say that you can be anything you want to be. Hannah could only say what she had vowed before God, which is "Your life will be dedicated to the service of the Lord." Samuel fulfilled the role of priest; he wore an ephod, anointed kings, and offered sacrifices. Hannah's fortitude and persistence paid off and Samuel's life pleased the Lord.

Chapter 7

Regaining A Lost Generation of Prayer Warriors

Chapter 7

Regaining A Lost Generation of Prayer Warriors

If one were to scan the women in attendance in our churches today, you will find a large majority of them inactive, missing in action, hiding as fugitives on the run, or just plain rebellious. There are generations of potential prayer warriors lost. Instead of chaste women training the younger women in Christ, the older women were teaching about a Christ who was endowed with their culture. Each subsequent generation has lost segments of truth and replaced the missing truth with humanistic traditions. Can the church regain its place of prominence in the world by refocusing its prayers and training the next generation? Will we again see powerful women moving from gossip to the gospel, and from displaying their personal opinions to dispensing biblical truths? As wonderful as a woman can be in her designed role, she can be just as deceptive and wicked when she moves out of it.

> *1 Tim 5:14 (KJS)* I will therefore that the younger women marry, bear children, guide the house, give none occasion to the adversary to speak reproachfully.

This is not a sentence by Paul for women to stay barefoot and pregnant in order to fulfill their purpose. The basic format for marriage, home, and how to conduct oneself is found in this scripture. Paul understood all too well the importance of women in ministry, but he also was aware of the fundamentals that must be adhered to in order to establish a healthy spiritual and marital life. If you trace most problems that exist in the church today, they will in most cases lead back to a woman. Please do not misunderstand my statement as implying that

71

men are not guilty of dissension and division. If Christian men would avoid the characteristics Adam displayed and surrender to the Holy Spirit's power to transform them into men like Jesus, the woman and the church would be better off.

> *Titus 2:2 (KJS)* That the aged men be sober, grave, temperate, sound in faith, in charity, in patience.
> 3 The aged women likewise, that [they be] in behaviour as becometh holiness, not false accusers, not given to much wine, teachers of good things; holiness:
> 4 That they may teach the young women to be sober, to love their husbands, to love their children, sober:
> 5 [To be] discreet, chaste, keepers at home, good, obedient to their own husbands, that the word of God be not blasphemed.

In the above passage of Scripture, Paul covers the proper conduct from the church house to the family house. He also accentuates the importance of the older women who should be spiritually teaching the next generation of women. If the aged women display the characteristics of a slanderer, backbiter, or gossiper, the younger women will exercise that same level of stupidity. We must stop the senseless gossip in churches that discredits and dilutes the power of the gospel. Thank God for the older praying women who embraced me and transferred to me their passion for prayer. I would rather have my mouth to God's ear than to Sister Hot News' ear. Instead of building up the body, the so-called-Saints seem to be destroying the body. Satan has successfully turned the mouths of could-be-prayer warriors into the launchers of missiles of destruction. The church desperately needs praying women interceding for the church and the pastor, and displaying a real concern for the church of Jesus Christ.

I have personally spoken to teenagers who called their parents hypocrites because they overheard them negatively feasting on their pastor for lunch. When the women of God speak negatively regarding their pastor, they send the wrong message to their children if they are overheard. Furthermore, they are programming the next generation of potential prayer warriors to undermine and disrespect God's delegated authority in the church. Woman of God, if your child is repeatedly saying that they can not wait until they reach eighteen so that they can leave the house, that is an indictment upon your character. What message are you conveying at home that would cause your child to choose to sleep out in the streets, rather than under your roof? Your standards cannot be double standards! The Bible says that a double-minded man is unstable in all his ways. It is impossible to have a wonderful spiritual life and your home not reflect your personal relationship with God.

Where are the strong Christian women whose daughters emulated them, husbands respected them, and sons adored them? I have always had strong women in my life who were apt to teach me the ways of the Lord. Mother Strait was one of those women whom I will never forget as long as the Lord keeps me healthy and vibrant. She took me in when I was only eighteen years of age and a soldier in the military. Her way of caring for me and treating me like I was her son was something that I will cherish for a lifetime. Her husband was not a Christian, but he highly respected her. While she was dying of cancer, I went to her bedside to tell her the good news that God had called me to preach. She called me closer to her in a whisper, yet with a motherly command, and asked for my Bible. As she clutched my Bible in her hand, she said, "Here's your Bible. Take it!" As I reached out to grab it, while she was still holding on to it, she said, "Son, God has entrusted His word to you to preach. Don't let the

Lord down. I'll see you in heaven." That most momentous occasion happened back in 1977. The many people that I lead today are experiencing her impact on my life.

I do not believe that praying women who are pouring out their soul to God can get up off their knees and use that same mouth to tear down their pastor, brothers or sisters. The book of James is explicit about the fact that it is impossible for sweet and bitter water to come from the same fountain. The lives of many women of the Bible are being used as preaching material in women's conferences, and as examples for how women should live their lives today, but not much of it is adhered to. What would Jesus' Mother say about you if she had an opportunity to view how you conducted yourself at home, church, or work? Mother Mary was a great woman before God selected her to become the mother of Jesus. She became even greater after she gave birth to Him. She did not allow gossip and accusations to hinder her purpose. She remained tenacious and focused. Her heart was set on doing everything possible to please her God. She was also included in the 120 people who were waiting for the outpouring of the Holy Spirit. I wonder whether it is difficult to see how important the woman is to the plan of God. Mary fascinates me because she went to

75

Elizabeth to share her news, only to discover that Elizabeth not only could identify with her joy, but also shared a similar experience. Their coming together was not to gossip, but to rejoice. As they were greeting one another, the baby inside of Elizebeth's womb leaped. The Son of God and John the Baptist were about to be born. These precious women were not simply giving birth to children; they were giving birth to ministries that would change the world. If a woman could only see that her life is an assignment that is holy and in her are prayers that can literally change situations. Mary had to be a woman of character and faith because the ultimate character and faith was residing in her womb. You can only produce after your own kind. If you are a prayer warrior, you can only produce prayer warriors. If you gossip and have double standards, you can only manufacture what you are. Become women of prayer and God will assign your prayers to change lives, and some child's future will be altered because you prayed. A child saved is a soul saved, plus a life!

Chapter 8

The Silhouette of a Woman:

The Missing Masterpiece

Chapter 8

The Silhouette of A Woman:
The Missing Masterpiece

I strongly believe that God is bridging the gap between church leadership and that which was lost in the area of prayer in the lives of women. Women have been systematically pushed into the backdrop and driven into the work force. My aim is not to disenfranchise or to eliminate the men from the picture of prayer. However, I can see the silhouette of a woman formed in the book of Genesis at the manifestation of the physical man. Most Bible scholars and serious students of the word would agree that, oftentimes, God has a message behind the message or a message within the message. Likewise, we can see in Genesis at the creation of humanity that there was another form inside of the Adam model. You cannot discover the beauty of the ocean by swimming on the surface. God is fully aware that if someone is hungry enough for knowledge, they will inquire or dig deeper by seeking Him. Those who will inquire of God will be allowed to see the message between the message. Within every story Jesus articulates, there is a message. Between every word God utters, there is a deeper revelation. Once you move beyond the surface, you will begin to see all the other things unfold. You can call it figurative, prototypical, or metaphorical; however, the truth remains that there is a face behind every mask, intent within every word spoken, and purpose stamped behind every activity. Humanity is just like its Creator. Women are a fine example of one hiding a message behind words and actions. Oftentimes, most men are confused to what their wives are looking for when questioned. If women will admit it, they will tell you that they are looking for their husband or future husband to inquire deeper into what was spoken in order to decode the message. And then they can discover what was really meant.

Gen 1:26 (KJS) And God said, Let us make man in our image, after our likeness: and let them have dominion over the fish of the sea, and over the fowl of the air, and over the cattle, and over all the earth, and over every creeping thing that creepeth upon the earth.
27 So God created man in his [own] image, in the image of God created he him; male and female created he them.
28 And God blessed them, and God said unto them, Be fruitful, and multiply, and replenish the earth, and subdue it: and have dominion over the fish of the sea, and over the fowl of the air, and over every living thing that moveth upon the earth.

Can you see the contours of the silhouette being formed?   Moreover, we will get a glimpse of something hidden in the man. Within the content of this passage of scripture is an appendix, supplement or sequel provided in order to draw the pattern or outline of a masterpiece. As you can see in verse 27 that although He [God] created him, in him [man]

80

was them [male/female]. God then blessed them, not just him. Please note verse 28 because there is a word used to describe a military activity. It is the word "subdue". This word means to demilitarize or to subjugate. That means that when God spoke into the make-up of man his design, He was informing him to bring something under subjection. Now, God will not give this kind of instruction unless there was something already here on earth, when He created man, that man would have to disarm.

Where was Satan at the creation of man? The Bible is explicit on the location of this infamous character. Satan was on earth before the creation of man and had previously lived in Eden the garden of God.

> Ezek 28:12 (KJS) Son of man, take up a lamentation upon the king of Tyrus, and say unto him, Thus saith the Lord GOD; Thou sealest up the sum, full of wisdom, and perfect in beauty.
> 13 Thou hast been in Eden the garden of God; every precious stone [was] thy covering, the sardius, topaz, and the diamond, the beryl, the onyx, and the jasper, the

sapphire, the emerald, and the carbuncle, and gold: the workmanship of thy tabrets and of thy pipes was prepared in thee in the day that thou wast created.

14 Thou [art] the anointed cherub that covereth; and I have set thee [so]: thou wast upon the holy mountain of God; thou hast walked up and down in the midst of the stones of fire.

15 Thou [wast] perfect in thy ways from the day that thou wast created, till iniquity was found in thee.

16 By the multitude of thy merchandise they have filled the midst of thee with violence, and thou hast sinned: therefore I will cast thee as profane out of the mountain of God: and I will destroy thee, O covering cherub, from the midst of the stones of fire.

17 Thine heart was lifted up because of thy beauty, thou hast corrupted thy wisdom by reason of thy brightness: I will cast thee to the ground, I will lay thee before kings, that they may behold thee.

The conveyance of this text goes far beyond the king of Tyre to Satan. The inconspicuous and invigorate ruler of all such pomposity and pride as that of the king of Tyre. Instances of this indirect reprimand to Satan are found in Genesis 3:14,15 and Matthew 16:23. There is more. The vision is not of Satan in his own person, but of Satan executing himself in and through an earthly king who arrogates to himself divine honor, so that the prince of Tyrus foreshadows the Beast.

Obviously Satan had access to the Garden of Eden and was probably watching God as He was creating and speaking to His new creation. Now that we can see the pattern unfolding, it becomes easier to understand why God commands the man to subdue the earth. There is certainly no reason to subdue plants and even animals because in their perfected state they were submissive to man. Why, then, does man have to subdue if the world did not have someone in it that needed subduing? Within this content of passage I can see the curves, contours and the framework being set as God is preparing the form, the mold, or the cast.

Excuse me as we take a brief advertisement to exploit the awesome design of the man. Before we can establish the intent of the glorious masterpiece, we must first procure a foundation. God does nothing without first developing a foundation. Jesus spoke about how important it is to have the structure on a foundation made of a substance of solidity. Whenever God initially started something, He instated the foundation with the male man. For some strange reason, our society is being desensitized toward the male gender. America and other nations are moving away from mentioning gender as though it has no real significance. Everything and everyone under heaven has a specific designed purpose before it was ever developed. Man became the foundation that God was able to build upon. Man is the glory of God just as the woman is the glory of the man. In other words, each was created or brought forth from its prototype or pattern. Consequently, the foundation is authenticated. It is inappropriate to have a structure without a substructure. The glory is what comes after or that which is placed on top of the foundation. Few people ever look at the Sears Tower, located in the city of Chicago, and find themselves awe struck of its foundation. The specimen of beauty is the structure.

When God decided to make man, the first physical specimen was the male man, not the female man. When God instituted kings over Israel, He selected male men. Please do not include the Judges because their position was not necessarily divinely appointed as Headship, but as a voice. The very sacrifices that God would demand from Israel were animals of the male gender. When God sent a Redeemer for mankind, He dispatched His Son Jesus. As Jesus was teaching His disciples to pray, His directions convened with "Our Father." Jesus elected 12 disciples who just happened to be male men. In fact, the Church itself is built upon the Prophets and Apostles. The reason why God initially selected men for the foundation structure is because the architectural monument tied to the foundation is the masterpiece of God.

The physical Adam was placed in this beautiful and spacious Garden, east of Eden. He had the sun, the moon, heavens, animals, a wonderful garden palace, and all the food he wanted to consume and yet God said that the man was lacking or under construction. Adam was not defective, but deficient. God was about to complete the process of man. It was God who said that it was not good that man was alone. Therefore, He provided a suitable and adaptable help meet. Someone who could help him meet the phone bill, electric bill, food bill, etc. (Smile)

Gen 2:15 (KJS) And the

85

LORD God took the man, and put him into the garden of Eden to dress it and to keep it.

16 And the LORD God commanded the man, saying, Of every tree of the garden thou mayest freely eat:

17 But of the tree of the knowledge of good and evil, thou shalt not eat of it: for in the day that thou eatest thereof thou shalt surely die.

18 And the LORD God said, [It is] not good that the man should be alone; I will make him an help meet for him.

19 And out of the ground the LORD God formed every beast of the field, and every fowl of the air; and brought [them] unto Adam to see what he would call them: and whatsoever Adam called every living creature, that [was] the name thereof.

20 And Adam gave names to all cattle, and to the fowl of the air, and to every beast of the field; but for Adam there was not found an help meet for him.

21 And the LORD God caused a deep sleep to fall

upon Adam, and he slept:
and he took one of his ribs,
and closed up the flesh
instead thereof;
22 And the rib, which the
LORD God had taken from
man, made he a woman, and
brought her unto the man.

It was in the Garden of Eden that Adam would learn how to dress and keep his wife by mirroring his activity and responsibility of the garden. Although God planted the garden, some items in the garden had to go through a growth process. Adam himself never experienced the process of growth because he was created in his mature form. There are two things we need to pay close attention to in v.21. One is that God only removed one "rib" from Adam to indicate their union. Secondly, the rib of the man was the substance from which God made the woman to indicate her position. The woman's position is not behind that man and she is not an afterthought of God. She was in the framework of the man. We also need to take note that God does not mention that the woman was directly made out of the same earth (dirt) from which Adam was formed. This is for a good reason. Adam's disposition with his wife would not be one of control or dominance. She was not formed to be a welcome mat on which he would walk as he would walk on the earth (dirt). She was the rib to indicate support and to rule by his side. The rib cage is one of the main bone structures to hold up and support the head.

I once heard a joke about how the woman is symbolic of the neck, which enables the head to turn. It may be so, but I say that the nerve impulses receive signals from the brain in the head in order to turn the neck in the direction the head wants to focus. Each gender has its divine purpose assigned by God.

Back to the subject at hand. I need for you to recall for a moment the location of Satan. Satan was in the garden and most likely saw that God formed this woman out of Adam's rib. Therefore, he must have understood God's reason for making this woman from a rib instead of the dirt. I believe that Satan captured the essence of the woman's design and knew that she would not and could not be independent of the man. Why do you think that Satan's attack on God's glory was through man's glorious help meet? In retrospect, the final dagger given to Jesus was a spear in the rib area. And to climax this revelation, consider the posture of the church. In Revelation 12:1-17, the church is the figurative woman who the devil tries to attack before she can bring forth the Man-child. When the devil discovers that the woman is divinely protected, he then goes after her seed. The devil has long known that the way to get at the man (seed) is to go after the woman. This awesome creation of God is the key factor in developing strength in the man's legs, fire in his desire, and the will to fight. Only then will the seed of the woman be in position to crush the head of the devil. Truly, the woman is the glory of the man.

Notice to whom the directions of God is given. God speaks to Adam because Adam is the leader, teacher and head. The first is always the foundation. Adam was placed first to lead, given directions by God in order to teach, and classified or ranked as the head so that he would be the responsible one. Eve repeated her lessons learned to the serpent in the garden, but she did not say it exactly as it was taught to Adam. Thus, Satan was able to deceive her and capture her power of influence over the man. It can now be easily seen that out of Adam was the masterpiece taken in order for God to complete what He originally said. "Let them have dominion..." is the consummation of authority. The assistant is usually the one with the influence, and the woman was created for this purpose. The curves, contours, framework, or silhouette was drawn for the woman at the same time God was making man. If the man does not treat this woman as God has designed, according to Peter, his prayers would be hindered. Therefore, the man needs to give to her all that God designed her to receive, his unadulterated love.

Chapter 9

Jezebel's Great Gift, Wrong Spirit

Chapter 9

Jezebel's Great Gift, Wrong Spirit

A prime example of a woman abusing her gift is Jezebel. Jezebel had tremendous leadership ability and was fully aware of her persuasive power. She was aggressive with her influence and she dominated and controlled people with fear. Her political power came from her husband Ahab who was the king of Israel. In those days, kings had absolute power and no one could contest them without the threat of dying. Although Ahab was the king, Jezebel ran the show. This authoritative woman exerted her power like a whip. No doubt Jezebel was demonically controlled because when she spoke people feared.

Jezebel, the wife of Ahab, king of Israel lived around B.C. 883. She was a Phoenician princess, daughter of Ethbaal king of the Zidonians. A pagan worshiper and supporter of the prophets of Baal. In her hands her husband became a mere puppet. Unable to think for himself and make decisions without employing the leadership of his wife.

> 1Kin 21:25 But there was none like unto Ahab, which did sell himself to work wickedness in the sight of the LORD, whom Jezebel his wife stirred up.

The first effect of her influence was the immediate establishment of the Phoenician worship on a grand scale in the court of Ahab. At her table were supported no less than 450 prophets of Baal and 400 of Eastward.

> 1Kin 16:31 And it came to pass, as if it had been a light

thing for him to walk in the sins of Jeroboam the son of Nebat, that he took to wife Jezebel the daughter of Ethbaal king of the Zidonians, and went and served Baal, and worshipped him.
1Kin 18:19 Now therefore send, [and] gather to me all Israel unto mount Carmel, and the prophets of Baal four hundred and fifty, and the prophets of the groves four hundred, which eat at Jezebel's table.

The prophets of Jehovah were attacked by her orders and put to the sword. Jezebel was a diabolical, merciless and devilish person. She cared about no one but herself and in maintaining her sphere of influence.

1Kin 18:13 Was it not told my lord what I did when Jezebel
slew the prophets of the LORD, how I hid an hundred men of the LORD'S prophets by fifty in a cave, and fed them with bread and water?

94

> **2Kin 9:7   And thou shalt
> smite the house of Ahab thy
> master, that I may avenge the
> blood of my servants the
> prophets, and the blood of all
> the servants of the LORD, at
> the hand of Jezebel.**

Jezebel is the kind of woman who will never look
to be married to a strong man. In order for her to be
empowered, she needs a wimp of a husband who
would look to his wife as his mother. When she found
her husband east down by his disappointment at
being thwarted by Naboth because Naboth would
not sell king Ahab his land, Jezebel arranged to have
Naboth killed so that Ahab would acquire the land
for free.

> **1Kin 21:7   And Jezebel his
> wife said unto him, Dost thou
> now govern the kingdom of
> Israel? arise, [and] eat bread,
> and let thine heart be merry:
> I will give thee the vineyard
> of Naboth the Jezreelite.**

Ahab was a poor excuse for a king and an even
worse example as a man! He would cry to her like a
baby and Jezebel would do anything to cheer him up

and to satisfy her personal need to be leaned on. She was the consummate mother/wife. She loved Ahab because he provided her with the need to be wanted. There are many women in the world of this same caliber who search the crowd to find people that are weak and in need of a motherly leader. However, Jezebel is not the kind of woman a person can easily manipulate or cross. This kind of personality can be very convincing because she sets up her prey with gifts and warmth. Little is her prey aware of the attachment that comes with those gifts and motherly warmth. If she said that she was going to get you what you want, you better believe it will be on your doorstep in the morning. Jezebel essentially told her husband not to worry about Naboth's land. Get up from your crying because I am going to bring you Christmas in July. Jezebel was Santa Claus making promises and delivering them on time. She wrote a warrant in Ahab's name, and sealed it with his seal. As you read the verses below you will see that the announcement came to her, and not to Ahab that the royal wishes were accomplished.

> 1Kin 21:8 So she wrote letters in Ahab's name, and sealed [them] with his seal, and sent the letters unto the elders and to the nobles that

[were] in his city, dwelling with Naboth.

1Kin 21:9 And she wrote in the letters, saying, Proclaim a fast, and set Naboth on high among the people:

1Kin 21:10 And set two men, sons of Belial, before him, to bear witness against him, saying, Thou didst blaspheme God and the king. And [then] carry him out, and stone him, that he may die.

1Kin 21:11 And the men of his city, [even] the elders and the nobles who were the inhabitants in his city, did as Jezebel had sent unto them, [and] as it [was] written in the letters which she had sent unto them.

1Kin 21:14 Then they sent to Jezebel, saying, Naboth is stoned, and is dead.

One day Elijah challenged the prophets of Baal to a contest to see whose God was real. The challenge was simple, make an altar and the God that answers by fire is the winner. Well, of course, the gods of the prophets of Baal could not as much as bring a spark. When it was Elijah's turn, he had the people to wet the altar and wood seven times. After his simple prayer to God had reached an end, Jehovah God answered by fire and the fire was so intense that it licked up the water in a second. At the instigation of Elijah, the people rose against Jezebel's ministers and slaughtered them at the foot of Mt. Carmel.

> 1Kin 18:40 (KJS) And Elijah said unto them, Take the prophets of Baal; let not one of them escape. And they took them: and Elijah brought them down to the brook Kishon, and slew them there.

Afterward, Elijah told Ahab to get up because he heard the abundance of rain. Elijah began praying for rain and the rain came just as Elijah, the true prophet, had said. When Ahab reached his palace and told Jezebel what had happened, she was angry. She concluded that her prophets were killed at the command of Elijah. God was not simply returning the favor of her killing His prophets; the people were only fulfilling the requirement of the penalty assessed when a false prophet is exposed. Although death was the penalty for exposing false prophets in Israel, Jezebel made a proclamation against a true prophet that she did not have enough power in her arsenal to fulfill.

> 1Kin 19:1 (KJS) And Ahab told Jezebel all that Elijah had done, and withal how he had slain all the prophets with the sword.
> 2 Then Jezebel sent a messenger unto Elijah, saying, So let the gods do [to me], and more also, if I make not thy life as the life of one of them by tomorrow about this time.
> 3 And when he saw [that], he arose, and went for his life, and came to Beersheba, which [belongeth] to Judah, and left his servant there.
> 4 But he himself went a day's journey into the wilderness, and came and sat down under a juniper tree: and he requested for himself that he might die; and said, It is enough; now, O LORD, take away my life; for I [am] not better than my fathers.

Elijah was God's premier prophet, who displayed remarkable power as no other prophet of his day. Yet, when he receives the message from Jezebel's messenger, he runs for his life. What made Elijah so afraid that he would forget about God's great ability to deliver him? Especially, after experiencing God consume a wet altar with fire without using two stones to create a spark. When Elijah regained spiritual consciousness, he went back to prophesying and fulfilling his purpose. He spoke what would befall the evil Jezebel and how dreadful it would be.

> 1Kin 21:23 (KJS) And of Jezebel also spake the LORD, saying, The dogs shall eat Jezebel by the wall of Jezreel.

> 2Kin 9:30 And when Jehu was come to Jezreel, Jezebel heard [of it]; and she painted her face, and tired her head, and looked out at a window.
> 2Kin 9:31 And as Jehu entered in at the gate, she said, [Had] Zimri peace, who slew his master?
> 2Kin 9:32 And he lifted up his face to the window, and said, Who [is] on my side? who? And there looked out to him two [or] three eunuchs.

2Kin 9:33 And he said, Throw her down. So they threw her down: and [some] of her blood was sprinkled on the wall, and on the horses: and he trode her under foot.

2Kin 9:34 And when he was come in, he did eat and drink, and said, Go, see now this cursed [woman], and bury her: for she [is] a king's daughter.

2Kin 9:35 And they went to bury her: but they found no more of her than the skull, and the feet, and the palms of [her] hands.

2Kin 9:36 Wherefore they came again, and told him. And he said, This [is] the word of the LORD, which he spake by his servant Elijah the Tishbite, saying, In the portion of Jezreel shall dogs eat the flesh of Jezebel:

I wanted to display Jezebel's history so that the reader can catch a glimpse of a totally corrupt heart and the misuse of her divine gift. Can you imagine if Jezebel would have surrendered to God how powerfully she could be used for God's glory? If she had that much power to incite her husband to perform evil in the sight of the Lord, what could she have done to influence Ahab to be a good king? She had a tremendous gift of influence, but she abused her gift and power and the corruptness of her heart led her to perform great evilness in God's sight and influenced others to do so as well.

Chapter 10

The Women of Deliverance

Chapter 10

The Women of Deliverance

Finding a woman who does not understand her position is like looking for a blade of grass. You can practically find them every where. It is very difficult to locate a woman who is not in competition with her husband and who fully respects and honors him as she would Jesus. Every woman must fight off the Eve syndrome, which is to be in charge. Her job is to influence, not take the lead. The serpent in the garden appealed to Eve's secret desire to be like God, knowing good and evil. Little did she know that she was already like God because she was created in His image; she just did not know all that God knew. Some things are reserved for God and God alone. Satan's plan was both calculating and intelligent. Satan knew whose ear to whisper in and what device to attract her with. Ever since the garden experience, the woman has displayed an irrepressible, enthusiastic desire for material things. The woman in the garden of Eden created the first debt. She wanted something that she could not have, but was willing to do anything to get it. Although she did not qualify for the fruit from the forbidden tree, it did not stop her pursuit of locating a co-signer. Satan was not after the woman; he simply used her to get to the man because the original authority was in the man. Delegation of authority comes from the leader, teacher and head. This is why after God made the woman from the rib of Adam that He brought her to him. Adam said this is bone of my bones and he, not God, called her woman (womb man). Even after their fall and banishment from the Garden, Adam called her Eve and that became what she would be known as.

Eve needed a co-signer for the debt that she could

not pay, so after biting of the fruit she gave to Adam, her husband, to sign by biting from the fruit. Ever since then, man and woman have been biting from forbidden items and enslaving themselves to Satan. She used her influence to weaken the man when she could have used it to strengthen him. When a woman is delivered from her irrepressible desire, she will use all her influence and resources to help the man.

> Luke 8:1 (KJS) And it came to pass afterward, that he went throughout every city and village, preaching and shewing the glad tidings of the kingdom of God: and the twelve [were] with him,
> 2 And certain women, which had been healed of evil spirits and infirmities, Mary called Magdalene, out of whom went seven devils,
> 3 And Joanna the wife of Chuza Herod's steward, and Susanna, and many others, which ministered unto him of their substance.

These women who attended the footsteps of Christ were opposed to the custom of Palestine. Their fusion of the sexes was not a common practice.

The rabbis held that the law should not be taught to women, yet Jesus allowed them to follow him and to encounter his teachings. Mary, called Magdalene was because of Magdala, a village near the Sea of Galilee. This is the first mention of her, and we know nothing more of her preceding history. We know that after her deliverance, she was one of the most devoted friends of Christ. Joanna was the wife of Chuza who held a very responsible position with Herod. Her husband Chuzâ, steward of Herod, is held by some to be the nobleman of John 4:46-53 "who believed and his entire house." She must have been a woman of wealth and influence because she was one who supplied Jesus' ministry with her substance (wealth). Not much is known of her, other than her assistance given. Susanna, who is not named elsewhere, contributed to his support. These women used their means to support Jesus and the apostles while preaching. The very fact that Jesus now had twelve men going with him called for help from others and the women of means responded to the demand. This is the first woman's missionary society for the support of missionaries of the Gospel. They had difficulties in their way, but they overcame these, and great was their gratitude and zeal.

Attention: **All Women and Mothers**

── The Praying Mothers Network ──

Join a network of praying women from around the world and capitalize on dynamic prayer secrets that will change your life.

Tire of the devil's meddling?

It's time to take back the control of your household by exercising your God-given gift of prayer influence.

Not only are you joining Mothers from around the world who are praying with you and for you, but these are some of the advantages of being a part of The Praying Mothers Network.

- **You will receive a FREE bi-monthly newsletter full of prayer secrets and stories of Mothers who are making a difference in their families and churches.**
- **Your name will be placed on a prayer list that will circulate throughout the world with praying Mothers just like yourself praying until change comes to your situation.**
- **You will receive discounts on all products offered through The Praying Mothers network.**
- **Your will receive a FREE tape entitled, "The Silhouette of a Woman" which exposes the power of a woman's influence.**
- **And Many More items**

To Sign-Up:
Call: **1-915-595-1307**
or *Write:* **1208 Sumac Dr. El Paso, TX 79925**
www.thepocketmotivator.com

OTHER BOOKS BY MIKEL BROWN

GOD'S REPOSITIONED MAN

The male man has a mandate on his life that must be encountered and satisfied for real fulfillment to pour into his life. The Man is so important to the delicate balance of the earth that one "sin" from Adam upset the entire earthly system.

This book was not written to encourage indifference towards the woman, but to reach the man that wants to change but doesn't know how.

Only $7.95

There is an infectious disease rapidly speading; destroying our strong and annihilating our weak. This book is designed to stop the continuous spread of this germ and to boost your spiritual immune system.

THE DISCERNMENT OF SPIRITS

There are three sources from which people give utterances and are motivated. They are the Holy Spirit, Satan, and the human spirit. The gift of Discernment of Spirits is designed to detect which spirit's motivation is in operation in order to protect the Body of Christ.

Only $7.95

To Order:
call (915) 595-1307
or write 1208 Sumac Dr. 6 El Paso, TX. 79925
www.thepocketmotivator.com

Power Communications Network

Empowering A Generation
Through Communications

Mikel Brown, CEO

"Life-changing" is the word to describe Mikel Brown's ability to articulate a message that is able to permeate the soul of a person. He is a well-traveled businessman, lecturer and author whose appeal is from sales to religion.

Mikel Brown's clients have included:

*K-Mart,

*Sul Ross University,

*University of Texas at El Paso

*and Evangelical Christian Leaders

For speaking engagements, seminars, conventions, business meetings, salesmen conclave, employee motivational work shops, or church conventions,

Please contact;
Pat Cruz
1-915-595-1307
or
www.thepocketmotivator.com

Notes

Notes

Notes

Printed in the United States
18659LVS00001B/114